For Virginia !

Stay awesome!

The Princess Who Saved Herself

Written by Greg Pak
Based on the song by Jonathan Coulton
Art by Takeshi Miyazawa
Colors by Jessica Kholinne
Lettering by Simon Bowland

www.gregpak.com • www.jonathancoulton.com
Published by Worldbuilders. Printed in Canada.

Once upon a time there was a princess named
Gloria Cheng Epstein Takahara de la Garza Champion

Who lived in a castle
by a waterfall

With a pink
and purple wall.

She ha
pet sn

And she ate a
whole cake...

...but mostly
she played guitar.

So did the very wicked queen
Who lived a mile down the stream

And who nearly lost her mind
Every time she heard the grind
Of the princess's red guitar.

And the bee grew twelve times bigger and let off a stinky smell!

But the princess loved all bugs! So she just gave it lots of hugs

And invited it to tea and music time.

So the witch banished the sun!

But the princess just had fun
With a campout, lots of marshmallows and friends.

The witch got quite irate.
(And in truth, it was quite late.)

And the princess kept on playing
with the clanging and the jangling

So the witch sent her blue dragon to
steal and burn poor Glory's red guitar!

But Glory turned on the garden hose
And she got him in the nose!

And she caught him by the tail!
And ignored his mighty wail!

And the witch's
forest burned

And Glory's
stomach churned

So she rode the dragon down to save the day!

But the witch was still so angry that she called the princess

The princess heard those mean words and they just made her

But deep inside the witch and princess both just felt so...

So the princess just said

And the queen began to cry
And said

Glory felt her stomach drop.
Like a bubble just went pop.
And she thought of what went wrong

And how on earth to change the song.

The queen just stood there in the breeze.

Then reached out with her long claws...

...and slowly tuned our Glory's red guitar.

Because she never knew that
her guitar could sound so great.

So they started up a band
And the dragon played the bass
And the princess showed the queen
How to put makeup on her face

And every day they play

And the kids come out to dance

Because sometimes everyone's a hero

If you just give her a chance.

Once upon a time there was a
princess named Gloria Cheng Epstein
Takahara de la Garza Champion.

She's my favorite kid

Honest, brave, and true.

But now that I look closely...

...I think she might be you.

The End.